The Winter Bird

Kate Banks

illustrated by Suzie Mason

CANDLEWICK PRESS

It WAS THE TIME OF YEAR when the sun went to bed early.

The big brown bear lumbered off to its winter den.

The hedgehog dove into its nest of moss and leaves under the shed.

And the birds prepared to fly south.

The geese were the first to leave, rising into the pale gray sky, followed by the starlings and the swallows.

Soon all had left but the nightingale who had broken a wing and couldn't fly. It watched from its nest at the base of a thicket.

"What will happen to me?" it sang sorrowfully. "I am a spring bird."

"You will stay here with us winter ones," hooted the barn owl from its perch.

"But I know nothing of winter," sang the nightingale, who was used to the feel of sunlight stroking its feathers and the warm breeze that rustled the leaves. It was used to drinking from the puddle pond and having plentiful food.

"You will learn," hooted the owl. "You will learn."

Little by little the cold crept in on icy feet. And the waltz of winter began.
It grew so cold that the puddle pond froze to glass. So cold that the chimney tops
began to spout smoke.

"What is that?" piped the nightingale when the first wet flake fell onto its back.

"It's snow," said the rabbit.

The flakes fell faster and thicker, burying the nightingale's nest.

"Where will I go?" it sang.

"Come in, come in," said the rabbit, who welcomed the songbird into its burrow and helped it to build a soft bed from dried leaves and twigs.

The nightingale crouched in the darkness, listening to its heart beating and wondering what morning would bring.

Winter plodded on and food became scarce. When there were no more seeds
and nuts to be found, the gray squirrel shared its stores with the nightingale.
And the woodpeckers gathered around the songbird, watching and waiting
for the bundled-up children to come out of their houses and fill the feeders.

The winter days passed, and little by little the nightingale grew used to the crisp crackling of branches and the crunch of snow on the footpaths.

It learned to forage for food on its own. It learned to stay warm, sheltered in snowdrifts.

And as the nightingale grew wiser in the ways of winter,
the winter creatures got used to the nightingale's song.

All was well until one day an eerie hush settled and the
world became muffled in silence. A blizzard was on the way.

The winter creatures rounded up
supplies and readied their homes.
And then they waited.

"What is a blizzard?" sang the nightingale, who only knew of summer squalls and spring rains.

"You will see," said the owl, who brought the nightingale some spare feathers to warm its wings.

The gray squirrel and the rabbit stuffed a nutshell with fur for the nightingale's feet.

Soon the world was awhirl in white.

"Oh dear," sang the nightingale as a flock of crows encircled it.

"Sing us a song," they squawked.

And the nightingale, who had always sung of summer's sweetness, began to sing of winter's woes.

But it wasn't long before it sang of winter's wonders.

The blizzard had covered the world in a shimmering blanket. Icicles dripped from the rooftops and windowpanes glistened with frost. Footprints dotted the landscape, along with snowmen and angels. And far beneath the snowdrifts were the first rumblings of spring.

Then one day the snowflakes were replaced by snowdrops. Green buds sprouted from the trees. The bear lumbered out of its den. And the hedgehog appeared once again.

The nightingale flapped its now mended wing.
"Goodbye, winter," it chirped. "Hello, spring!"
And as the other creatures looked on, the nightingale
puffed out its chest and rose into the air, singing joyfully.

It was a spring bird, but it had become a winter bird, too.

For my sister Amy
KB

For Richard and Rupert, for always
SM

First edition 2022

Library of Congress Catalog Card Number pending
ISBN 978-1-5362-1568-7

22 23 24 25 26 27 APS 10 9 8 7 6 5 4 3 2 1

Printed in Humen, Dongguan, China

This book was typeset in ITC Slimbach.
The illustrations were created digitally.

Candlewick Press
99 Dover Street
Somerville, Massachusetts 02144

www.candlewick.com